Ruben's Bag…A Ruben Kane novel

I0684819

Other Books by this Author

Enlisted at 14…A Memoir

Enlisted at 14…And the Journey Continues

Willow…A Novel

Just a Dream

Willow…and the Medusa

Enlisted at 14…Looking Back

Meet Ruben Kane

Willow…One for the Team

R. K.

Book 3 of the Ruben Kane Series.

The Fellows ... Remembrance

I often think about my childhood, the kids I grew up with, and the six square blocks we ran around in and called our own. I even believe I can remember many of their names, like Little Bit, Kochi, Lawrence, and Nikki to name a few. I'm sure there are still a couple hanging around that same old block, looking for a dollar. I miss those guys, although I wouldn't want to go back for love nor money. However, you wonder how they're doing and how they turned out. All doing well, I hope, all prospering.

Ruben's Bag

By

Eddie J Martin

Part 1

"I told you I know nothing about what you are talking about; if I knew I'd tell you."

The person I was speaking to was a short fellow of about five foot two and weighed approximately 110 pounds. He was part of Cleveland's drugs and numbers gang. I could have cleaned the floor with him but the two men with him caused a problem for me, plus I was bound to a straight back chair in somebody's basement.

The little man had hit me on the head several times and I felt it. It reminded me of when I was a kid when there was always a little guy with larger guys telling him to, "Slap him, Shorty." And Shorty would do it if they were there. However, fast forward to now and while Shorty had grown up, he was still short, and the boys were still behind him saying, "Slap him, Shorty." Some things never changed.

These guys were after drugs and money (what else) in a laundry bag. Someone they were chasing tossed the bag in my car, without my knowledge, as I got a haircut. I drove away and these guys found out what the thief had done and came after me. They caught up with me a couple of days later, covered my head, and brought me to the basement in this house. Whoever put the bag in my car must have come back and gotten it or somebody got it because I don't have it. It was August so I had my windows down so anyone could have put the bag in it and taken it out without my knowledge.

"We know that the fellow we were after tossed the bag in your car, someone saw him. You left the area but when we did find out whom you were, there was no bag. So, my friend, where is my merchandise?"

"I'm telling you," I said. "I never saw a bag in the back of my car; I had no reason to look back there anyway."

"Okay, okay. Let's say we believe you and you do not have our bag, but you can find it for us. You see, we know who you are and what you do is find things. You're Ruben Kane, the private dick who lives on the lower West Side with a wife named Ella. So, we want you to find our bag."

"If you know all this about me, why did you grab me? And hell, if you can't find it how do you expect me to?"

"Don't know, don't care how you do it, just find it," Shorty said.

"I usually am paid for my work," I said.

"How about this: we won't kill you if you find our bag but we will kill you if you don't. Is that payment enough?"

"Sounds good to me," I said.

Two hours later, they let me out at the Cave club at 79th and Cedar on the east side of Cleveland. They told me whom they suspected had their drugs and how they got on to me. It seems like the guy they were chasing was on foot and passed by the barbershop where I had my car parked with my windows down, which gave him the opportunity to take the bag.

"We were close on his ass but not close enough. We checked around and someone saw him toss the bag in your car. It took a while, but we found out whom the car belonged to—you! The guy may have known you and that's why he picked your car or it may have just been coincidental."

So was the abduction just to get my attention? Well, they did. I dragged myself into the club, sat at the bar, and ordered a JB on the rocks.

The bartender looked at me and said, "Hey, RK, you don't look so swell, bad night?"

"Yeah, you could say that, Tank, better make that a double."

The club was only partly full since it was a Monday night around 9 PM and things didn't start happening until at least 11. I wasn't looking for no action, just to rest my bones and figure out how in the hell I was going to get out of this one. I picked up my drink and walked over to a table so I could stretch my legs. I noticed they hadn't gone too hard on me otherwise they would have had their heavies take a crack at me. And Shorty had said something about my face hurting his fist. Hell, they knew I didn't have their damn drugs or even if I did, I wasn't foolish enough to keep 'em. You see I knew the old boys, or know of them anyway, and there was nothing to play with. I'd never had a run in with them until now, so I believed them when they said they'd blow me away if I don't come up with the bag. Coincidence, that's all it could have been, as no one knew I was going to be at that barbershop at that time of night, I didn't even know it. Therefore, that's out, but then again, it's not as if anyone knows my car. If so, he could have easily followed me home or to my office and retrieved the bag. Let me backtrack a little. Shorty told me that the bag was lifted from their car, which was parked in the alley. They spotted the thief and when he started running with the bag they took off after him on foot. He cut around a corner and they lost him. Now, when they did make the corner he was nowhere in sight. However, they did pass a barbershop, massage parlor, grocery store, and cleaners. They glanced in each one but didn't see the guy so they moved on. There were several cars on the street, and they said that they looked in a few but found nothing but evidently, they didn't look in mine. Now, I left the barbershop around 8:30 PM Saturday night. I picked up my girlfriend Freda around 10:30 PM after stopping by my apartment and taking a shower. I remember seeing a few guys coming in the shop, but guys come in the barbershop all the time, either looking for someone or seeing how many more customers the barber has before their turn. So, I paid little attention to them, since I was already in the chair. Once I got out, I said "next time" to Raymond the barber and went to my car, which was parked a little way down the block. I never saw the runner with the laundry bag, but Shorty said he was a tall, six foot three, lanky, bald-headed black guy of about 150 pounds. As they never found someone that looked like that, I guess it was better to put me under the gun. I called the waitress over to order another drink and then I asked her to call me a cab.

The next morning, I walked in my kitchen and found my wife Ella sitting at the table having coffee.

"Hey, what are you doing here?" she said.

"I live here," I said.

"I haven't seen you in a while," she said. "I was beginning to wonder if you still lived here."

Ella and I had an understanding: she had a friend that she saw quite often and I had a lady friend I was fond of. We both met at breakfast and coffee some mornings, that was when I was not staying over at my friend's and she was not at hers. Why we stayed together only God knew, but we managed to see each other at least two or three times a week.

"Any coffee left?" I said. "That bacon sure smells good."

"Look," Ella said, "why don't I just fix breakfast for you?"

"Would you do that for me?" I said.

"Sure, why not," she said.

"Thanks, I'll save money by not going to the diner this morning."

"Yeah, Ruben, I sure know how you like to hold on to that dollar."

"Every little bit helps," I said. "Now if they just did something with those gas prices. $0.28 a gallon is way too much for gas."

"I hear they're talking about even selling water in the future," Ella said.

"That'll be the day," I said. "You done with the sports section?"

"You know I'm not into sports, Ruben," and she handed me the paper. "What case are you working on now, anything interesting?"

"Not a thing, Ella, seems like I hit a dry spell," I said. "I'm sure something will pop up." I didn't tell her about the latest bullshit I'd gotten myself in.

"You never stay idle for very long," she said.

"You're never wrong about that," I said.

Part 2

Rita was sitting at her desk doing her nails at 10 AM in the morning—what else was there for her to do? Rita was a lady of Mexican descent, 26 years old, five foot two and just as wide. She had shoulder length black hair and was cute as hell. Did I mention that she talked plenty of shit? She was an illegal that'd been in the States about five years now and had been working for me half of that time. I really couldn't afford a secretary, but the price was right. On the other hand, I couldn't afford the office either but again the price was right. I had done a service for a banker and his family a while back and to show his appreciation he'd rented me this office space for a dollar a month on a 20-year lease.

"Any messages, Rita," I asked as I walk past her going into my office.

We only had the two rooms: the outer, which is the lounge, consisting of a desk with a phone, filing cabinet, leather couch, two lounge chairs, two end tables with lamps, and a floor table for magazines. One door led into my office where there was a bathroom, desk, a chair that faced my desk, one hat rack, and pictures on the wall of Billy Holiday, Charlie Parker, and Coleman Hawkins. A window behind my desk looked down on Main Avenue in Cleveland's Central Park. You could see the trolley cars going by in each direction but being up so high, on the 13th floor, you never heard them. I loved that view!

"Raymond called and said he needed to talk to you ASAP or sooner. Sounds important," Rita said.

"Well, it may be but not before my coffee and nip." Did I say I was hooked on coffee plus the nip?

Rita bought my coffee and I reached in the bottom desk drawer and pull out my half-full bottle of Jim Bean, poured two fingers in the cup, leaned back in my armchair, put my feet up on the desk, and took a sip of the liquid. Nice! If I didn't watch myself, I would become an alcoholic but I think it was the coffee I most appreciated.

"What's up Raymond? You called."

"RK, what kind of shit have you gotten yourself into this time? A few of 'those guys,' and you know who I'm talking about, came by asking questions like they were Johnny law or somebody about a tall, bald-headed black guy and you."

"What did you tell them, Raymond?"

"Everything I knew, RK, which wasn't much. I know those old boys and they're nothing nice. They must have believed me when I told them that you were in the barber's chair when all of this went down, but they kept on asking me questions about you and I guess a light went off in the short one's head and he said he had heard of you. Then he mentioned that thing with Tonelli and the bullet last year. I'm sorry, RK, but I couldn't lie to those old boys as they play rough."

"It's okay, Raymond, everything's cool for now. By the way, did you know whom they were talking about when they mentioned a tall, black, bald man?"

"Not a clue, maybe he's from out of town, but I'll keep my eyes and ears peeled. If he's smart, he'll get the hell out of this area especially looking like that."

"Yeah, you're right. Raymond. I'll be talking to you. I hope he doesn't leave before I get my hands on him as my life depends on it."

I decided to call a cop I knew at the Cleveland Police Department and see what information I could drag out of him. Detective Jeffries sometimes told me things and sometimes he wouldn't, depending on what I had for him and how he felt that day.

"Detective Jeffries? Ruben Kane here, how you doing?"

"What is it, Kane? I don't have a lot of time, especially for you."

"Why are you acting like that, detective? Don't I always help you when I can?"

"What do you need, Kane, hurry it up."

"Have you gotten information on any new people coming in from out of town?"

"Be specific, Kane, what the hell are you talking about?"

"For instance, a tall, black, bald Negro?"

"No! But then again, I haven't been looking for anyone like that. Why are you looking for this person? Anything that concerns me?"

"I don't think so, detective, he has something that belongs to someone and they hired me to find it for them."

"You want to tell me what this something is you looking for?" Jeffries asked.

"Not right now but maybe later," I said.

"I'll keep an eye open," he said. "Now, what do you have for me?"

"What are you looking for?"

"There has been a rash of break-ins over on the lake area; we think it's a team of two. A Negro male and a white girl aged 24 and 26 respectively. They have gotten away with at least $75,000 in jewelry and furs. They hit only high-class homes. We're stumped."

"Okay, detective, I'll see what I can find out for you and keep an eye open for Baldy for me, will you?"

"You got it, Kane."

Demon C. Turret, a.k.a. Baldy, was sitting in the Cleveland City Jail and had been there since Saturday night. Right after he dropped off that bag in the Buick, he hightailed it through the back alleys until he came across a bicycle, rode it to Main Avenue, and cut across the street. That's where the cops stopped him for jaywalking and joyriding on a bicycle. He tried arguing with them but they thought he was just trying to be smart and took him to jail. He still had to explain the bike. It being a weekend he knew he'd have to stay locked up at least until Monday, maybe even Tuesday. And, with little money for bail, he may have to do more time than that. He'd almost had his hands on the big one, watching Theo's old boys leave that bag in their car. He had a hunch there could just be a little something in there that he could use. Where he came from, Negros that looked like that were only up to three things: picking up numbers money, payoffs, or drugs. It didn't matter to Demon if he could get some of it. He'd been on a streak of bad luck lately and that's why he had left Kansas City (KC). After he lifted the bag, looked in it, and saw the money and drugs, he felt that his luck had changed. That's when the men had come out of the building, spotted him, and the bad luck continued.

"Shorty! You got a collect call from the city jail, you want to take it?"

"City jail!" Shorty said. "Any of our people got picked up lately?"

He was told they hadn't.

"Yeah," Shorty said.

"Shorty, this is the pigeon, remember me?"

"Yeah, what is it, Pigeon? I guess you need someone to help you get out of jail."

"Yeah, that would be nice, Shorty and after I tell you this little bit of information that may help my case."

"I'm listening," Shorty said.

"I hear you're looking for a tall black guy about six foot three from out of town. This guy was picked up Saturday night, get this, for jaywalking. He just got into town from KC and has been here the week. I think this may be your boy."

"Sounds like him, Pigeon. Get me his name as he'll be getting bailed out along with you. $125,000 in cash and at least that much in drugs, looks like I'm getting closer," Shorty said.

"Rita, why you so down in the dumps this morning?"

"RK, you know life is a bitch, it's just not fair."

"What is it, Rita, is it anything I can help you with?"

"No, not with this one, RK, no one can help me with this one except the federal government maybe."

"What are you talking about, Rita?"

"It's my cousin, Haze, the government picked him up at his job, and now they are going to deport him. He has two little girls depending on him. Who is going to take care of them?" she said. "It's just not right."

"Where is his wife?" I asked.

"She was killed coming across the border, it's just not right."

"Who will take care of the kids now that the dad is gone?" I asked.

"Relatives or friends or someone, I guess; you know Mexicans are close-knit that way. Someone will take care of them," Rita said. "Why! Why!"

"Why what, Rita?" I asked.

"Why would a big country like this want to deport my cousin? He's just a little person. It's not like they don't have room enough in the country for him. Mr. Kane, let me ask you something."

"Shoot, Rita," I said.

"If you saw a few Mexicans coming across the border looking for a better life for themselves, their family and their future, what would you say to them?"

I looked at her, knew she was serious, and wanted a straight answer so I said with the straightest face I could conjure, "Well, I'd say, welcome home amigo, welcome home."

"Thanks, RK, I needed that."

"Oh, by the way, you got a phone call from Joel's pawnshop and he needs to talk to you."

Joel's was a pawnshop I'd had dealings with from time to time. You see not all pawnshops were created equal. Some pawnshops got merchandise they were not supposed to have and they knew it. However, because of the money, they wanted to keep it. If they called the cops, they knew it'd be a never-ending thing and every time something came up missing, they'd come around harassing them. The bottom line was they wanted to keep the merchandise and not get busted too.

"Ruben, I got this couple been coming in the shop now for six months with some damn good merchandise. I will admit to you I'm making some pretty good bread and I hate to lose it but these people are getting a little too hot. I'm reading in the paper lately they're hitting wealthy homes and I think they're getting a big head. I'm afraid if they get caught they're going to say where they have been getting rid of the stuff."

"So, what exactly do you need from me, Joel? Call the cops, you can do that yourself."

"I want you to do what you do, Ruben, you're good at that."

"You're not talking about bumping them off are you, Joel? I'm not into that."

"No, Ruben, nothing like that, although that isn't a bad idea but no, nothing like that. Just get rid of them, make them disappear. Run them out of town. Hell, you know what I'm talking about. Ruben, you do this for me and I'll be willing to give you up to $500."

"I'll tell you what, Joel, for you I'll do it for $1000; 500 up front and you don't question how I get the job done."

"That's a deal, Ruben, how soon?"

"The cops have been after these people for months, Joel, so give me at least a week. When can I pick up the 500?"

Thursday 10:30 AM

"Ruben, this is Detective Jeffries, we may have found the bald guy you been searching for."

"That's great," I said. "Where is he?"

"In an alley off 69th and Harriet Street all beat to hell; looks like he's been tortured. Both legs are broke, three fingers cut off one hand, burns over half his body, and one eye out. He's a mess. Unbelievably he just got released from the city jail Tuesday; someone bailed him out. You want to tell me now why you were searching for him?"

"Well, detective, it seems like he took something from someone and they wanted it back and hired me to locate it for them. Looks like I lost on both counts."

"You want to tell me who your client is?" Detective Jeffries asked.

"You know I can't do that," I said.

"You may have to, this is a murder case now."

"Ruben, Ruben, how you doing? I was sitting at the bar at the cave club when Shorty and his crew walked in."

"Hey, Shorty, fancy meeting you here," I said.

"How you going finding my money?" Shorty asked.

"I'm still looking, Shorty, I'm getting close to this baldhead dude, shouldn't be long now."

"Is that right," Shorty said.

"Yeah, Shorty, I'm on the job."

"Don't waste your time looking for Baldy, I found him, and guess what, Ruben, he doesn't have my money so that means we're back to you."

"You found Baldy?" I asked. I knew that he had but I had to play dumb.

"Yeah," Shorty said. "And I do believe him when he told me he didn't have my money. Number one. He doesn't have my money. Number two. He doesn't know where my money is. Number three. Somebody has my money and gonna give it up. Right now, I feel, you, Ruben Kane, have my money so until you prove otherwise get me my mother-jumping money. You have two days."

"Now, Shorty," I said. "Be reasonable. You know damn well I don't have your money."

"Two days, Ruben, two days."

After Shorty and crew departed the club, I wondered to myself just how in the hell I was going to come up with that money. Hell, I didn't even know how much money it was. I'd been in fixes like this before and came out okay and I should be able to do the same this time. Shorty had pretty much told me they'd put it to Baldy. If I couldn't find that money somebody was going to get a nickel call on him to Detective Jeffries. Not that I was a snitch, mind you, but pressure can be a mother.

Part 3

2482 Lake Wilson Drive, Friday, 24 August 1938, 9:30 PM.

Jake and Carla rowed up to the pier and tied up the two-person kayak. The night happened to be the darkest of the month. They were wearing all-black wetsuits. Carla had to wear boot black over her face and hands to cover her white skin but Jake was good, being a Negro. The Bradys, whose home they were going to burglarize, were out at a benefit fund of which they were chair and co-chairman. The benefit was given once a year and had been held for the past 10 years on the same date and same time for approximately three hours. This function was highly publicized and one of the highlights of the year. It included Tommy Dorsey's Big band orchestra featuring the Andrew Sisters. Judges, the mayor, lawyers, celebrities from newspaper and radio, and also a few movie stars. The highlight of the occasion would be the governor of the state showing up. Anyone that was anyone would be at that event.

The rear of the home was approximately 100 yards from the water and the dock. Even though there were lights, Jake and Carla managed to shoot several out with a homemade slingshot. A cabin cruiser was tied up with a light on it but they left that one on. Ten minutes later, they were in the house and going through the Brady's master bedroom and closets.

Jewelry was laid out in plain view and by chance, the safe was left open. Furs, which they didn't take this time, but everything else, they could carry in their bags. Diamonds were found in the safe along with cash, gold, and silver coins. After taking everything they could find and carry, they departed the same way they entered, through the lower floor bathroom window.

I was sitting on the hill above the homes on Lake Wilson Drive. I knew of the benefit held there every year and that the people in this area were all members. I had a hunch this would be a good time for the thieves to act. The benefit started at 8 PM and would finish at 11 PM so he surmised that if there was going to be a hit it would have to be between those hours. I arrived on the hill a little after eight and sat down to wait with my spyglass in hand. There were three to four homes I could watch from this location; the Brady's were at the top on his list but I could be wrong. At 9:30 PM, I thought my eyes were playing tricks on me. I noticed that a light went out on the boat dock. I thought nothing of it at first and then it happened again on the same dock. It was at the Brady's residence. Out of six lights, four had gone out.

This really got my attention and I focused the scope on the dock. That's when I noticed two figures arrive in a two-person kayak and head for the rear of the house. I didn't see them enter but I knew they did. After 25 to 30 minutes, they departed and returned to their kayak carrying two large bags.

Jake and Carla pulled away from the pier for about 200 yards and then veered right parallel to the beach and moved away from Cleveland. I knew of several areas they could pull in but the thing was working out which one. Since there was no moon, I got into the Buick and tried as best I could to follow them. They traveled up the coast for approximately five miles and pulled into a small cove that the kids used as a Lover's Lane that was also a boat ramp. But since it was only around 10:30 PM, no one was around. The couple made it to the beach and pulled the kayak out of the water, Jake had parked their Jeep nearby. Driving it around to the water, they loaded the kayak on the roof and put the bags inside. Changing out of their wetsuits to shorts, tank tops, and sandals, they prepared to leave. It was about half a mile from the cove down a dirt road to the main highway and that's where I saw them. If it wasn't for the kayak on top of the Jeep, I would have missed them. On seeing them, I made a U-turn and started following.

I followed the Jeep to a little town 20 miles outside of Cleveland. They turned into a farmhouse with a long driveway leading up to the house. A wooden fence off the road. I parked on the outside and watched them go in carrying the bags. I waited 15 minutes and walked up to the house and around to the back. There was a window partly open so I looked through. The couple was jumping up and down and congratulating themselves. The loot was on the kitchen table and out of the bags and contained cash, jewelry, gold, and silver coins. They were elated. They both undressed and went in the back room; my guess was to make love, take a shower, or both. I thought I'd just wait to see if there was anyone else around. Twenty minutes later, they came out of the back room, each wearing a towel around their middle. From the fridge, the woman pulled out a bottle that looked like champagne. They toasted each other, they embraced, kissed, and lay down on the floor and after a lot of foreplay, they made love. Now, I really didn't need to see that and started to break in right there but never let it be said that Ruben Kane was heartless. So, I sat down underneath the window and waited. Later, I looked through the window again and saw they were lying on their backs with arms over their eyes breathing hard. The woman had her legs stretched out straight and the man had one leg bent at the knee and the other stretched out with a big smile on his face. It was about time to shake them up a bit, as all things must end. I eased over to the back door and tried the knob; that's one thing about living in the country and small towns—the doors are never locked. It opened and I quietly walked in. I stood over the two of them with my 38 in hand before I said, "Good evening!"

They both were startled and raised up on their elbows. The guy was more shaken than the girl. She was just looking for something to cover herself. The guy just laid there shaking and started to get up until I raised and shook the pistol at him.

"Who the fuck are you?" he asked.

"Never you mind about that, I know who you are. You two have been very busy tonight. What was that home number? Eight or ten? You should be in real good shape by now, moneywise that is."

"Okay," Jake said after getting his courage back, "what do you want? I don't think you're no cop."

"No, I'm not a cop, I'm worse than a cop. Tonight, I watched you rob a home in the lake area of Cleveland. You have all the booty from the house right here on the table."

"Like I said, what do you want?" Jake said.

"I want you out of here tonight. I don't care where you go, just go. Never come back to Cleveland again."

"And if we don't go?" Jake said.

"I call the cops right now, or I may just blow both of your asses away and take all the loot for myself."

Carla forgot about covering up and listened to what I said. She now said, "Give us an hour and we'll be out of here. That's what you want, right?"

"That's right," I said, "that's what I want. And oh yes, there is one other thing."

"What's that?" Jake said. "The cash you took from the house, I want it."

"Just the cash," Jake said.

"Well, you may want to toss in a few of Theo's diamonds too," I said. After leaving the house, I parked a little way up the road in a batch of trees. I stayed in the car and counted the money, which was a little over $20,000, and watched the house until Jake and Carla packed up their belongings and drove away.

The next morning, I gave Rita her pay plus a bonus, walked over to my desk and reach for the Jim Bean. By that time, Rita had put my coffee cup down.

"Rita, would you get Joel's pawnshop on the line?" I asked. When the call was answered, I said, "Hey, Joel, Ruben Kane here, how's it going?"

"I hope you have some good news for me, Ruben; I hear a home in the lake area was hit last night and of all people the Brady's. All hell is going to break loose now as those people are at the top of the ladder of their community. You think it's our two people?"

"I'm sure of it, Joel, but you can be sure of one thing: they won't be bothering you or anyone else in the area again, and the cops will never find them."

"You didn't knock them off did you, Ruben?"

"Hell, no Joel, nothing like that. All you need to know is that they're out of your hair."

"Ruben, I believe you and I trust you if you say they're out of my life. I'll be sending over your money plus a bonus. And thank you again, Ruben."

Now, what to do about the good detective? What should I tell him about my two friends? Should I tell him that I located them? Should I tell him that I also let them go? That's not a hard decision to make, no, no, and no. That'll be two that got away. But I do think I will have to give him a bone. I'm thinking that bone will have to be Shorty and his crew. Next, I need to find out where they hang out; that shouldn't be too hard. Most people in the hood know where they're at; it's kind of a well-known secret. One more day and he'll be coming after my ass and I still don't have any idea what Baldy did with that money. But I'm sure after Shorty finished with him he would have given it up if he knew. In 24 hours, I could trade with Shorty if I didn't find the bag. I figured I had something like $75,000 in total.

There was the $20,000 cash, the diamonds, and a few thousand dollars I had stashed away not to mention the Buick. I hated to get rid of it but it was new. I wasn't sure how much was in the bag but at least I had something to bargain with now if it came down to that. Ass before cash, that's what I always said.

Part 4

At 11:30 PM that night, I headed for the cave club to beat the bushes when I came across some kids singing at the corner of an alley. I stopped and listened to them as I often did sometimes. There were four of them; a very tall young man who I assumed was the bass, a smaller person who had to be the baritone, a third who was the second tenor and a fourth young man who was the youngest, smallest and the lead. After I parked, I

pulled my pint of Jim Bean out from under the front seat, popped the top, and took a hit right from the bottle. The group started up with the bass in spoken words: "You can take your L.A. women, your San Diego beaches and your Frisco piers, sunny nights, fires, and mudslides. The seasons are where I wanna be, Cleveland is heavenly to me…" And then the group came in with, "Cleveland is the place that I want to stay, Cleveland is my home in every way. Take your West Coast and East Coast too, if you haven't been to Cleveland then you really haven't flew. Drop me off in Cleveland, drop me off at home."

After the mini-concert, I headed for the cave club. It was Saturday night and packed. A band was playing the latest songs and it was wall-to-wall with men and women in their latest styles, dancing and covering the floor. As always, I spoke to those I knew, kissed the women, and shook the men's hands. I asked questions about Baldy to whomever I could and to whoever knew anything. I wanted to know when he came to town, who he knew, and who he partied with. The only thing I could find out was that he was from Kansas City and he was run out of town for having light fingers. I wanted to know how he ended up in Cleveland. I learned he used to live here as a kid. The family moved to KC at age 15 so he had knowledge of Cleveland and probably still knew a few people here. After finding out all I could at the cave club, I thought I'd head for the Ebony club, Tonelli's old joint. It was under new management, of course. It was also packed with a live band, dancing, and wall-to-wall with people. I went through the ritual of kissing the ladies and saying hello to the guys. One woman I knew very well told me Baldy was picked up outside the jail and taken to a building on the Upper East Side. I asked her if she knew the location of the building. She said she'd rather not say. After three drinks and an hour and a half later, I eventually convinced her to tell me its location and promised her we would get together later.

On Sunday morning, the first thing I did after getting off the couch was to call Rita and tell her not to come into work for the next few days. I figured Shorty would be calling on me and the office would be his first stop and the apartment would be his second. I didn't know if he knew about Freda but I assumed he did. So, I'd call her too so she could go over to one of her friend's houses for a few days. I couldn't get a hold of Ella, so I figured she was still out. I sure hoped Shorty didn't catch her at home. The next call was to Detective Jeffries but before I could call him, he called me.

"Ruben, I was hoping I'd catch you at the office. I guess I'm not the only one that works on Sundays."

"I guess not," I said. "What's up?"

"The Bradys got hit Friday night for quite a bit of money and jewels; we think it's the same two that have been hitting all the others."

"How did you let that happen, detective? Didn't you have it covered?"

"There's only so much we can cover, besides they had that damn benefit and most of my people were there. The rest of my men were spread out too, including the lake area. We were making routine checks but we can't be everywhere. We think they came in from the lakeside; we found lights out on the dock and they made their entrance through an open bathroom window. It didn't help any that I overheard Mrs. Brady

saying she thought she left the safe unlocked. I guess

that won't bother them though as rich folks are

insured."

"How much did they get?" I asked.

"The tally isn't in yet but if I had to guess I'd say quite

a bit."

"How are you going on the case? Doing any good?"

"None," I told Jeffries, "plus you know that's not my

side of town anyway. I know about as much as you, but

there is something I may be able to pass on your way. It

kind of makes the robbery case a little less stressful."

"And what would that be, Ruben? I need some good

news after all I've been through. I've got the chief,

District Attorney, and mayor on my ass over this one."

"You doing any good on Baldy's murder?" I said.

"It was my number one case until the robbery but yeah, we still on it."

"I may be able to help you there." I went on to tell him about Shorty's bag of goodies, Baldy lifting it out of his car, and Shorty and his crew taking chase and losing him. Then I explained how Shorty hired me to find Baldy and the money but I had found neither one. I told him that when Baldy got himself arrested that weekend, Shorty found out where he was and bailed him out, tortured, and killed him. "Of course, I'm just hypothesizing. Whether he found out where the money was, I don't know."

"You wouldn't happen to know where I could find Shorty, would you?" Jeffries asked.

I gave him the address that I had received and told him to be careful when he picked him up because he always kept at least two men around him and they were always heavily armed. He was also known to have drugs and policy numbers money in the house. "He's one badass, detective, better watch yourself."

"From what you've told me, it sounds like Shorty's my man. Thanks, Ruben. I owe you."

After I hung up with Jeffries, I thought, that went well. What I told him was mostly the truth and I hoped that now it'd play out just as well. It was time for me to make myself scarce.

On Monday morning, Detective Jeffries pulled up beside me while I was getting gas and asked, "How are you doing, Ruben? How much gas does that baby take? Looks like a lot. Private detective work must pay well for you to be riding around in a brand-new car."

"It's not bad, detective, when you retire you should try it," I said. "You seem happy this morning, detective, rich uncle die and leave you a bundle?"

"Pretty close, Ruben, we caught up with Shorty Sunday night but things didn't go so well for him. It seems like he and two of his boys tried to shoot it out with us and they didn't make it."

"That's too bad," I said.

"We think the gun we took off Shorty was the same one that put a round in Baldy's head; we'll know for sure after ballistics. You know, Ruben, the way you described Shorty you would think that he would have been six foot tall but, he was only five foot two. Was that a mistake on your part or what?"

"Well, tell me this, detective, how large was the pistol he held in his hand when he was trying to shoot you?"

"Good point, Ruben, good point. Thanks again for the info," he said.

"Don't mention it," I said. I looked Jeffries in the eye and said again, "Really, don't mention it!"

On Tuesday morning, Ella and I were both at home. Before leaving for the hairdresser she said to me, "I put your laundry in the laundry room but I never did get a chance to wash so if you need your things you'll have to wash them yourself."

I looked up at Ella from the kitchen table and said, "What laundry are you talking about?" as Freda had been doing my laundry for the last few months.

"The laundry you had in the back seat of your car. When you came in Saturday night, I borrowed the car while you were in the bath. I was only gone for 10 or 15 minutes and noticed the laundry bag in the back seat.

So, if you want the things in there washed you will have to wash them yourself."

"Where is the bag now, Ella?"

"In the laundry room in the basement in the laundry basket."

Our basket is a 10-gallon tub with a lid over it and the number of our apartment is on the side.

When Ella had closed the door and left, I said to himself, could it be? Was it that simple? Had Ella found the bag?

I ran down the stairs to the basement and the laundry room. I located the laundry basket and raised the lid. At first, I couldn't see the bag until I moved a few articles of clothing and there it was. It was a large canvas bag tied with a drawstring. I opened the bag and there it was: more cash than I'd seen in all my life, tied in bundles. In addition, there was some white

powder in packages that I assumed was cocaine.

"Well, I'll be damned," I said. "I'll be damned!"

The End